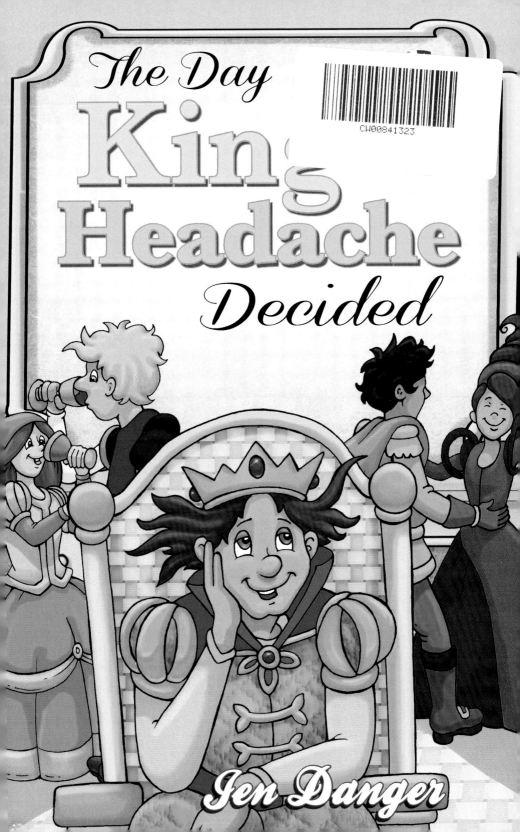

Published by Tate Publishing & Enterprises, LLC
127 E. Trade Center Terrace | Mustang, Oklahoma 73064 USA
1.888.361.9473 | www.tatepublishing.com

Tate Publishing is committed to excellence in the publishing industry. The company reflects the philosophy established by the founders, based on Psalm 68:11,
"The Lord gave the word and great was the company of those who published it."

Book design copyright © 2013 by Tate Publishing, LLC. All rights reserved.
Cover and interior design by James Mensidor
Illustrations by Jason Hutton

Published in the United States of America

ISBN: 978-1-62024-978-9
1. Juvenile Fiction / Social Issues / Self-Esteem & Self-Reliance
2. Juvenile Fiction / Social Issues / Friendship
13.07.10

Dedication

For Finley Grace;
here for such a time as this.

King Headache of X-Land was the richest king in the whole world—and he knew it! He threw an extravagant party just to show how rich he was. Everyone was invited; no one was excluded, from the most important, his advisor Mr. Grudge, to the very least, the janitor, whose name nobody knew.

King Headache wanted to show off his beautiful wife, Queen Bella, to everyone. He was the richest man with the biggest empire and he had the most beautiful queen! But Queen Bella was angry.

All the servants have gotten silly from too much chocolate and too many fizzy drinks. I certainly do not want to parade around like I am a show horse! thought Queen Bella.

Queen Bella disobeyed the king's orders and refused to go to the disco. Little did she know the unfortunate consequences to her decision.

I'm so embarrassed that Queen Bella did not come after I have bragged about her to everyone! thought the king. Mr. Grudge warned him that if people found out, King Headache would be the laughing stock of X-Land.

"Why don't you make a law, so no one can defy you anymore?" said Mr Grudge.

"Anyone who defies you will be chased away, starting with Queen Bella this very day."

King Headache agreed. Queen Bella was chased away and never heard from again.

After several sunrises, King Headache felt quite lonely. He missed his Bella, and wished he hadn't chased her away so rashly! He never ever knew what to do. His advisors always, well, advised him! Now it was too late, because once a law had been written in X-Land, it could never become unwritten. King Headache became as grumpy as he was lonely. Mr. Grudge was at his wit's end.

"Oh dear, what are we to do?
King Headache is in such a stew!
He's beginning to blame all of us,
and he is causing such a fuss.
Let's hold auditions to find a new queen,
the finest that X-Land has ever seen."

The advisors hurriedly told of their idea to put on a talent show to find a new queen. King Headache agreed, and the "X-Factor" auditions were the talk of the town. Girls came from everywhere hoping to be picked.

There was a girl who lived in X-Land called Estelle. Her parents had gone to heaven when she was quite small. Her Uncle Morty had adopted her, and Estelle had been his daughter ever since. Uncle Morty and Estelle were from a far away land called the Kingdom of Cariad. The Kingdom of Cariad had been a beautiful and mystical place where everything was made out of chocolate! But the Cariads had had to flee the Kingdom of Cariad when on a hot, sunny day the chocolate melted and all the walls tumbled down. Even though they now lived safely in X-Land, no Cariad could bear to eat chocolate—it just brought back too many memories from the Kingdom of Cariad. Unfortunately, the people of X-Land did not like the Cariads. The X-ers just could not understand why those Cariads wouldn't eat chocolate. Honestly, who didn't like chocolate? In fact, the X-ers thought that those Cariads were rather strange and stuck-up.

When Estelle went to audition for the "X-Factor," Uncle Morty warned her not to tell anyone she was from the Kingdom of Cariad. He was afraid if they knew the truth, they wouldn't like Estelle because of where she was from. That just would not be fair! He didn't want anyone to judge Estelle before they got to know her. Estelle listened to Uncle Morty's advice and kept her Cariad identity a secret.

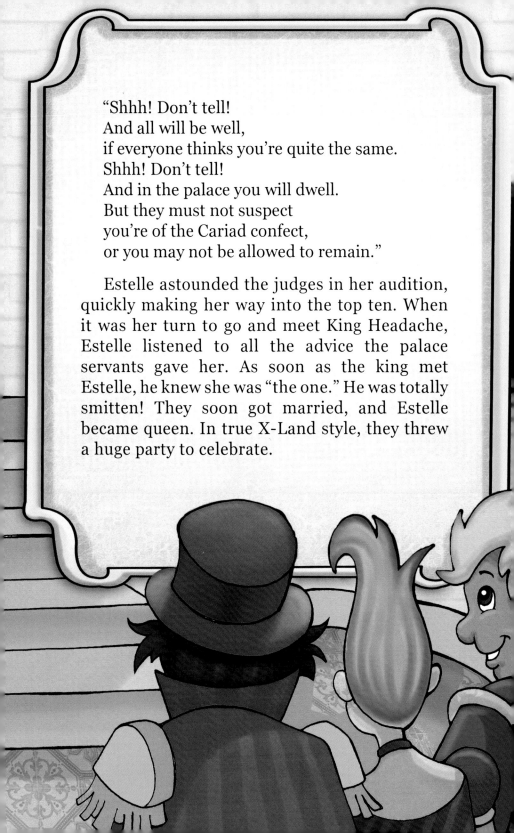

"Shhh! Don't tell!
And all will be well,
if everyone thinks you're quite the same.
Shhh! Don't tell!
And in the palace you will dwell.
But they must not suspect
you're of the Cariad confect,
or you may not be allowed to remain."

Estelle astounded the judges in her audition, quickly making her way into the top ten. When it was her turn to go and meet King Headache, Estelle listened to all the advice the palace servants gave her. As soon as the king met Estelle, he knew she was "the one." He was totally smitten! They soon got married, and Estelle became queen. In true X-Land style, they threw a huge party to celebrate.

Uncle Morty was over the moon for Estelle. He knew she would be very happy in the palace with King Headache. Uncle Morty lived nearby and would pop over for a cup of tea from time to time. One day, on his way home, he caught a terrible troublemaker outside the palace. The terrible troublemaker was up to no good and out to make trouble, but Uncle Morty managed to stop him. Reporters caught wind of what had happened, and the heroic story of Uncle Morty was all over the newspapers. Everyone was so happy that he had saved the day; they even made Uncle Morty into an action figure!

Mr. Grudge, King Headache's advisor, didn't like Uncle Morty. He was jealous of all the attention that Uncle Morty had gotten from the newspapers. It should have been him! He was who everybody should be talking about. But no, no one appreciated all the hard work that he did. Uncle Morty had tea and cupcakes with the king and queen while he had to do the dirty work of washing the dishes.

Mr. Grudge really wanted to chase Uncle Morty away and out of X-Land so that he wouldn't have to watch Uncle Morty having fun with the king and queen all the time. But he had to have a reason. Mr. Grudge devised a wicked plan to try and turn the situation around. He deliberately teased Uncle Morty when he saw him, especially if a police officer was around.

Mr. Grudge hoped that Uncle Morty would become angry and react and get into trouble. But Uncle Morty would never retaliate because, in the Kingdom of Cariad, his mama had taught Uncle Morty that even if someone was really, really, *really* annoying, they should be shown respect. Uncle Morty refused to take the bait, and Mr. Grudge became more and more irritated. He wished he could make up a reason to chase him away. One day, Mr. Grudge found out that Uncle Morty was from the Kingdom of Cariad.

"Perfect! What a brilliant way to disguise my plan.
Not only Uncle Morty, I'll chase away the entire clan.
Those Cariads are rather strange and stuck-up.
They don't even like chocolate!
I'll tell the king they're not very nice.
I'll even say they have head lice.
After all, they keep tight-knit,
and it's obvious they don't really fit.
Maybe they are even plotting
to see X-Land crumbling and rotting!"

Mr. Grudge told King Headache lots of big, fat lies about how terrible, awful, and horrible those Cariads were. He told the king that they should make a law to chase all the Cariads away from X-Land. King Headache, who didn't have a clue and didn't really know what to do, agreed and signed the law. The date was set that soon the X-ers would chase all the Cariads from the land.

When Uncle Morty found out, he was devastated. He knew exactly why Mr. Grudge had done this. It was to punish him. But now, not just him but all the Cariads would suffer! Where would they go? How would they survive? No one knew the way back to the Kingdom of Cariad, and they couldn't live in all that melted chocolate anyway. Besides, this was their home now! The situation required urgent action. Uncle Morty went to find Estelle straight way. He told her everything and asked her to try to change the king's mind.

"But Uncle Morty, if the king finds out
I'm a Cariad,
he might think I'm bad! I'd be sent away too.
What good would that do?"

"If we're sent away and never seen again,
what do you think would happen to you then?"
Uncle Morty replied.
"Though the X-ers want us dumped,
I know somehow good will triumph.
Don't be scared, for you've committed no crime.
You have been brought to the palace for exactly this time.
Be true to who you are, and your
goodness will shine through.
Tell the truth and King Headache is sure to believe you."

"You're right. I must go.
What will happen, I do not know.
One thing is certain: I must do what is right.
So I won't run away. I will stay here and fight.
I'll go to the king and tell him I am a Cariad.
I'll tell him that Mr. Grudge has lied and said we are bad.

I hope he will believe me and understand,
and King Headache will let us stay in the land."

Estelle cooked the king's favourite dinner that night and invited Mr. Grudge along. Mr. Grudge was beaming. Finally he'd been invited to have dinner! His pride pretty soon turned into fury when along the way he saw Uncle Morty. He couldn't wait until the day came when all those Cariads would all be chased away.

Later on in the evening, King Headache sat down to read the newspaper. He had decided that it was about time he found out what was going on in his own land. Estelle had been such a good influence on him. She often brought home the newspapers and always encouraged him to take an interest in matters and make his own decisions. On the front page of the newspaper was a photo of Uncle Morty! King Headache read with fascination about how Uncle Morty had saved the palace from the terrible trouble of the troublemaker. Wow! King Headache had had no idea! He called in Mr. Grudge.

"Mr. Grudge, my advisor, advise me! What would be a good reward for someone I really wanted to say a big thanks to?"

Mr. Grudge grinned and puffed out his chest. The king had finally noticed just how dazzlingly brilliant he was. Now he was going to make sure he got the best prize ever!

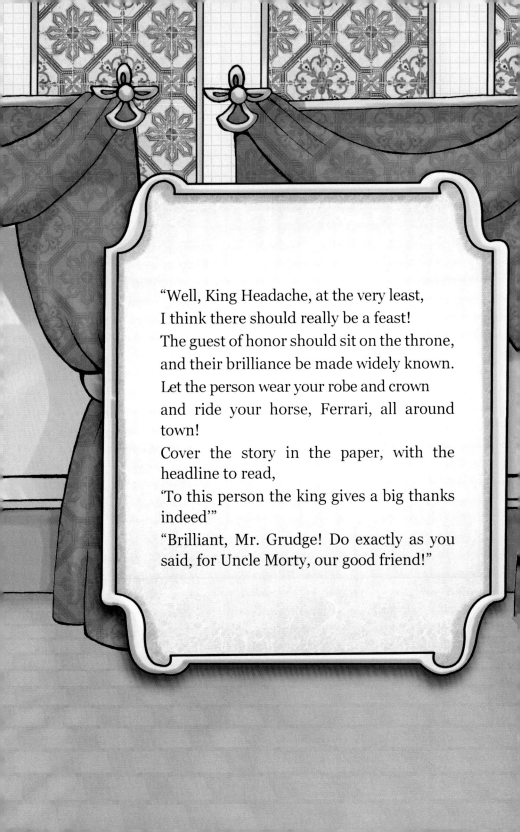

"Well, King Headache, at the very least,
I think there should really be a feast!
The guest of honor should sit on the throne,
and their brilliance be made widely known.
Let the person wear your robe and crown
and ride your horse, Ferrari, all around
town!
Cover the story in the paper, with the
headline to read,
'To this person the king gives a big thanks
indeed'"
"Brilliant, Mr. Grudge! Do exactly as you
said, for Uncle Morty, our good friend!"

Mr. Grudge was flabbergasted! He stood frozen to the spot, too dumbfounded to say anything. It wasn't him after all that the king wanted to say a big thanks to but awful Uncle Morty. Mr. Grudge was furious and full of scowls as he sat Uncle Morty on the throne, put a crown and a gown on him (the oldest and ugliest ones he could find, mind you!), and took a picture for the newspaper. People were positively pumped for Uncle Morty now that he had appeared in the newspaper twice. He had to give autographs out left, right, and center. Mr. Grudge was ready to explode with envy as he made his way back to the palace. He cheered up considerably when he was requested to have dinner with King Headache and Queen Estelle again. Soon his plan would come into action, and at last Uncle Morty and those horrible Cariads would be chased away and never heard from again in X-Land.

At dinner that night, King Headache could tell Estelle was troubled.

"Estelle, darling, what troubles you?
I hate to see you sad and blue."
Queen Estelle answered, "Please, don't chase me away!"
"What? Chase you away?
Estelle, my queen, you are here to stay!
I learned my lesson, and never again
will I send away my queen and friend.
Who would make such a terrible threat?
These words they will live to regret!"
said King Headache.

"Mr Grudge has been very naughty," said Estelle,
"all because he doesn't like Uncle Morty.
He told you that we're not very nice,
and even that we have head lice.
He even hinted that we are plotting
to see X-Land crumbling and rotting!
King Headache, it is simply not true.
Mr Grudge has lied to you."

King Headache couldn't believe his ears! Mr. Grudge had tricked him into signing the law. But what could he do? Everyone knew that once a law had been written in X-Land it could never become unwritten. One thing was certain: he had learned his lesson. No longer would he always ask others to make his decisions. That was day that King Headache decided. He issued a new law that said that if anyone tried to chase away the Cariads, that the Cariads had full permission to chase them back in the Battle of the Chasers. King Headache fired Mr. Grudge, and Uncle Morty became the king's advisor.

When the day of the Battle of the Chasers arrived, Mr. Grudge and his family were all geared up to chase. They certainly were going to give their best shot at chasing Uncle Morty away. The chasing began, and soon everyone teamed up to chase Mr. Grudge and his family from X-Land. They were chased away and never heard from again.

All was well that ended well, and the X-ers and the Cariads lived happily ever after. King Headache and Queen Estelle held parties every year to celebrate and remember the triumph of good over evil. They played chase-tag, held "X-Factor" auditions, and ate just the right amount of chocolate and fizzy drinks—along with good servings of fruit and veg, of course!

e|LIVE

---

listen|imagine|view|experience

AUDIO BOOK DOWNLOAD INCLUDED WITH THIS BOOK!

In your hands you hold a complete digital entertainment package. In addition to the paper version, you receive a free download of the audio version of this book. Simply use the code listed below when visiting our website. Once downloaded to your computer, you can listen to the book through your computer's speakers, burn it to an audio CD or save the file to your portable music device (such as Apple's popular iPod) and listen on the go!

How to get your free audio book digital download:

1. Visit www.tatepublishing.com and click on the e|LIVE logo on the home page.
2. Enter the following coupon code:
   686b-b495-c541-df56-7bcc-d41d-19b2-b01a
3. Download the audio book from your e|LIVE digital locker and begin enjoying your new digital entertainment package today!